You can be a
Brownie Girl Scout, too!

If you are 6, 7, or 8 years old, or in the 1st, 2nd, or 3rd grade, just ask your parents to look in your local telephone directory under **"Girl Scouts,"** and call for information. You can also ask your parents to call **Girl Scouts of the U.S.A.** at **1-(212) 852-8000** or write to 420 Fifth Avenue, New York, NY 10018-2702 to find out about becoming a Girl Scout in your area.

For Jilly, the best sister
in the world—J.O'C.

For Lisa and Charlie
and the new baby—L.S.L.

Copyright © 1994 by Girl Scouts of the United States of America. All rights reserved. Published by Grosset & Dunlap, Inc., a member of The Putnam & Grosset Group, New York, in cooperation with Girl Scouts of the United States of America. GROSSET & DUNLAP is a trademark of Grosset & Dunlap, Inc. Published simultaneously in Canada. Printed in the U.S.A.

Library of Congress Cataloging-in-Publication Data

O'Connor, Jane.
     Lauren and the new baby / by Jane O'Connor ; illustrated by Laurie Struck Long.
         p.   cm. — (Here come the Brownies ; 6)
     Summary: Lauren is excited at the prospect of a new baby in the house, but her best friend Marsha is afraid it will spoil their friendship.
     [1. Babies—Fiction.   2. Friendship—Fiction.   3. Girl Scouts—Fiction.]
     I. Long, Laurie Struck, ill.   II. Title.   III. Series.
     PZ7.0222Lau   1994
     [E]—dc20   93-44879

ISBN 0-448-40467-2 (pbk.)   A B C D E F G H I J

ISBN 0-448-40468-0 (GB)   A B C D E F G H I J

HERE COME THE BROWNIES
A Brownie Girl Scout Book

Lauren and the New Baby

By Jane O'Connor
Illustrated by Laurie Struck Long

Grosset & Dunlap • New York
In association with GIRL SCOUTS OF THE U.S.A.

1

"It's so cute and little. It looks like it belongs in front of a dollhouse," Lauren said. She squatted beside the tree—a tiny pine—that her Brownie Girl Scout troop had just finished planting in McCormack Park. The girls had bought the tree with money saved from returning a grand total of 763 empty soda cans and bottles.

Lauren put down her shovel and pushed her glasses up on her nose. "It's just the cutest thing," she said again. "Our very own little baby tree!"

Marsha, who was Lauren's best friend, groaned. "You know what? You've got babies on the brain!"

Lauren shrugged. It wasn't the first time that Marsha had said that. But it was true. Lauren couldn't deny it. In a few weeks Lauren's mother was going to have a baby. And it was practically all Lauren could think about. She was going to be a big sister. At last!

"Last week my brother said he'd take Lauren and me ice-skating," Marsha announced to no one in particular. "But *noooo*. She wanted to help paint the baby's room instead."

Marsha acted like she still couldn't believe it. But then Marsha didn't think a new baby was any big deal. Of course, Marsha already had a little sister as well as a big brother. She didn't understand that being an only child sometimes got lonely.

Lauren thought her parents were great. But being around just grown-ups wasn't always fun. Half the time they didn't even get Lauren's jokes. And the house was too— Lauren tried to put her finger on it—too peaceful. It was always so nice and busy over at Marsha's house.

Lauren looked up as Mrs. Quinones, their

troop leader, passed out animal crackers for snacktime.

"I know it's hard to believe this tiny tree will ever be big. But I guarantee it," Mrs. Q. said. "One day our tree will look just like that tree over there." Mrs. Q. pointed to a tall pine. "I planted that tree with my very first Brownie troop. Fifteen years ago! Long before any of you were even born." Mrs. Q. sat down and fanned herself with her hat.

"You mean it's going to take *that* long for our tree to grow up?" Lauren said.

Mrs. Q. nodded. "Sometimes the most special things are the ones you have to wait the longest for...like the new baby."

"Yes, I know," Lauren said. "But waiting is so hard." Lauren was a girl who liked things to happen fast. She talked a mile a minute. She was the fastest runner in 2-B. She was a quick reader. She even ate fast. "You know we're not timing you," Mom would tell Lauren almost every night during dinner.

Marsha, on the other hand, could make a lollipop last practically forever, licking it *sloooowly*, until it was so thin you could see right through it. And if Marsha liked a book, she'd read it extra-slowly, so it wouldn't end. In fact, in most ways really, Lauren and Marsha were exact opposites.

Lately, 2-B had been studying antonyms. Antonyms were words that were opposites. Like *big* and *little* ... *hot* and *cold* ... *young* and *old*. And lately Marsha and Lauren had been calling themselves the Antonym Twins.

Marsha loved playing with dolls and doing gigantic jigsaw puzzles with about a trillion pieces. But Lauren didn't have patience for any of that. Marsha liked ballet dancing, while Lauren loved sports like soccer, where you had to move—FAST! Lauren practically lived in jeans or leggings. Marsha nearly always wore dresses. Lauren loved pepperoni pizza. Marsha hated it.

On and on it went. Still, Lauren liked being with Marsha best of any of her friends. They always thought up big, interesting projects to do together. They ran a lemonade stand together at the tennis courts across the street from Lauren's house. They were fixing up the old tree house in Marsha's yard. And they loved playing Monopoly games that lasted for hours.

Lauren thought about all this as she finished her last animal cracker—a giraffe. Then she joined the other girls who were gathering around Mrs. Q. under the shade of a big, flowering tree.

"So, tell me. How is everybody coming along with their newspaper articles?" Mrs. Q. looked around the group. "Remember, we're meeting on Sunday at my house to go over our first drafts."

The Brownie Girl Scouts were trying to write a newspaper about all the things they had done during the year. It was called *The Troop Tribune*. The idea had been Amy's. Her father worked for the town paper. He

wrote about people who had just died—
"obituaries" was what Amy said they were
called. After the Brownie newspaper was all
done, it was going to be printed. It would
be given out at their school and to all their
families.

"I started writing about the camp-out,"
Jo Ann said. "That was my favorite thing."
She turned to Amy, who was having her
hair braided by Corrie. "Amy, I hope you
don't mind, but I put in the part about your
throwing up after the cookout."

Amy giggled and shrugged. "No
problem!"

"I'm writing a movie review," said Krissy
S. Krissy S. loved movies. She wanted to be
an actress someday.

"I think I'm going to write about our
visit to the day-care center," Lauren said. "I
got to feed and burp one of the babies."

Lauren still remembered how the baby had curled its fat little fingers around her pinkie. It had felt so nice.

Marsha groaned again and looked around at all the Brownies. "See! What did I tell you? She really does have babies on the brain!"

Lauren giggled. "I can't help it! Honest!"

"Well, I want to do an advice column," Amy announced to the group. "You know, where people write in with questions and problems and I try to answer them. Just like the 'Dear Abby' column in my dad's paper. Only I'm going to call mine 'Dear Amy.' So if anybody has a problem, just come to me. I promise not to tell a soul." Amy pretended to zip up her lips.

By now it was almost the end of the meeting. Several parents' cars were pulling into the entrance of McCormack Park. So

Mrs. Q. quickly gathered the troop in a circle around the tiny pine tree.

Everyone crossed arms, held hands, and began the friendship squeeze. The Brownie Girl Scouts ended almost every meeting this

way. It was Lauren's favorite part. She passed the squeeze from Corrie's hand on one side of her to Marsha's hand on the other.

From Brownie to Brownie, all the way

around the circle, went the friendship squeeze. It reminded everyone how they were all sisters. Sisters in Girl Scouts. That always made Lauren feel proud and special. And soon she was going to be another kind of sister. The big sister of some little baby. Lauren was hoping it would be a girl. But a boy wouldn't be so bad, either.

Lauren smiled to herself. So what if nobody else thought being a big sister was a big deal. It still filled Lauren with the proudest, most special, good-from-the-toes-up feeling ever.

2

Lauren was sprawled out on the floor of the den with a notepad and a bunch of sharpened pencils. She was trying to start her newspaper story for *The Troop Tribune*.

It was Saturday morning and very quiet in the house. Daddy was out jogging. Mom was still in bed.

"Didn't have a great night's sleep, honey. Going to snooze a little more," Mom had muttered groggily when Lauren popped in to kiss her good morning.

More and more her mom was having trouble sleeping. And that was hard since her mom was still going to work every day. Her father and mother were both tax accountants. They shared an office downtown.

Lauren tapped her pencil eraser against her teeth and read over what she'd written. So far, so good:

OUR DAY AT A DAY-CARE CENTER
Our Brownie Girl Scout troop visited the Lots of Tots Day-Care Center. We helped with the babies. It was fun.
I got to hold a baby and burp it. The baby spit up on me a little. But I did not mind all that much. It did not get on my Brownie sash.

Just then the phone rang. Lauren leaped to get it before it woke up her mom.

It was Marsha.

"I was just trying to write my newspaper story," Marsha told Lauren.

"Me too."

"But I can't decide what to write about."

Lauren giggled. That was nothing new. Marsha could spend hours in front of a candy counter just trying to decide what flavor chewing gum to pick.

"Listen," Marsha went on, "my parents got a new rug for the living room. And my mom says we can have the old one for the tree house. We can cut it down and make it into wall-to-wall carpeting!"

"Cool!" Lauren said. Lately, she and Marsha had been spending most of their lemonade stand money on posters and curtains for the tree house. They liked to

pretend that they were
grown-ups with jobs,
sharing an apartment
together.

"So when can you
come over?"

"Well, not for a
while, actually," Lauren
answered. "I'm waiting
for my dad to get home.
We're all going to pick
out a crib and some
other stuff for the baby.
Hey! Why don't you
come with us? It'll
be fun."

There was a little
pause. Lauren thought she
heard Marsha sigh.

GiRLS
ONLY

"That doesn't sound like so much fun to me," Marsha said. "Do you have to go shopping for baby stuff?"

"No," said Lauren truthfully. "But I want to. Come on, Marsh. Come with us. *Pleeease*!"

Usually, it was pretty easy for Lauren to get Marsha to change her mind. But this time Marsha wouldn't budge.

"Well, I guess I'd better get off now," Marsha said. "Maybe I'll call Corrie. Or Jo Ann. Maybe one of them will want to come over and help me cut down the rug."

Wait a sec! Lauren had always thought of the tree house as sort of their own private place. Why couldn't Marsha wait and do the carpet later? she wondered. Why did it have to be right now?

"Well...okay...if that's the way you

want it," Lauren said. She tried to sound as if it were perfectly alright with her. "Fine."

"Fine," Marsha echoed.

Then they both got off the phone. They didn't really hang up on each other. But they didn't really say good-bye, either.

Lauren looked at the phone. Had she and Marsha just had a fight? And if they had, what had it been about?

* * *

The trip to the mall was not as much fun as Lauren had hoped. They had to wait forever to pay for the baby things. And the whole time Lauren was thinking about the maybe-it-was, maybe-it-wasn't fight with Marsha.

On the ride back, they had to drive right by Marsha's house. Lauren tried to look the other way. But she couldn't help seeing

Marsha out of the corner of her eye. She was leaning out of the tree house to help pull Jo Ann inside.

"Hey, there's Marsha and Jo Ann," Dad said. "Should we drop you off so you can play with them?"

"No, don't bother," Lauren said. She slunk way down in her seat so the girls wouldn't see her. Maybe it was stupid and babyish. But Lauren couldn't help feeling left out.

Mom shot Lauren a funny look. "What's this all about?" she asked.

"I'm not sure," was all Lauren said.

It was the truth.

Finally, that evening, Lauren decided to call Marsha. Maybe tomorrow after the Brownie meeting Marsha could come over and play. Maybe by then everything would be back to normal between them. But when Lauren called, Marsha wasn't home. She was at the movies with her father and brother. "She won't be home until quite late, honey," Marsha's mother told Lauren. "But I'll tell her you called."

After Lauren hung up she felt worse than ever. The movie Marsha had gone to was one they had talked about seeing together. How could Marsha have gone without asking Lauren to come, too?

3

Early Sunday morning, the phone rang in Lauren's house. That has to be Marsha, thought Lauren, calling to say she's sorry she went to the movie without me. But it wasn't Marsha. It was Mrs. Q. And she had some sad news. One of Sarah's hamsters, Louie, had died during the night.

"Oh, poor Sarah," Lauren said. Sarah had about a zillion pets. And she was crazy about all of them.

"Some of the girls wanted to go over to Sarah's house to cheer her up," Mrs. Q. explained. "And Sarah told me that she would like that. Can you meet there about two o'clock this afternoon? We'll postpone our newspaper meeting until the regular troop meeting on Friday."

"I'll be there," Lauren promised.

Sarah lived only a few blocks away in the same development. So a little before two,

Lauren's dad walked her over.

Many of the other Brownies had already arrived. But Marsha was nowhere to be seen. Where was she? Lauren wondered.

Sarah was in the living room with her puppy Muffin on her lap. Her cat Norma was asleep at her feet. Sarah wasn't crying. But her eyes looked red and puffy.

Sarah's two remaining hamsters—Huey and Dewey—were in their cage, burrowed in

a nest of wood chips. Lauren wondered if they had any idea that Louie was gone.

"How did Louie get sick?" Amy asked. "I mean, I hope it's okay to ask."

"It's okay. My dad doesn't know, and he's a vet." Sarah held out her arms and shrugged sadly. "This morning I found Louie in his cage. Just lying there. We buried him out front," Sarah said. Each of the condos in the Shady Acres development had its own small yard. "I'll show you where."

Everyone trooped outside.

Lauren looked at the little mound of dirt beside some bushes. There was a popsicle stick stuck in it, with "LOUIE" written in capital letters going down the stick.

"Louie was lucky, if you ask me," Corrie said. "If I were a hamster, I'd definitely want to belong to you."

26

Several of the other girls nodded.

"Why don't we sing something for Louie?" Jo Ann suggested.

Everybody liked that idea.

"How about 'Taps'?" said Krissy S.

Yes! "Taps" was about things coming to an end. The girls had sung it at the close of their last campfire. So the troop clasped hands and started to sing,

> "Day is done.
> Gone the sun
> From the lake,
> From the hills,
> From the sky.
> All is well,
> Safe at rest,
> God is nigh."

Lauren looked around the group. Practically everybody in the troop had shown up. Except Marsha. I wonder why? thought Lauren. That wasn't like her.

For a moment, Lauren thought about calling Marsha when she got home to find out the reason. But no, she decided. She'd called Marsha last night when Marsha was off at the movies. Now it was Marsha's turn to call her.

When she got home from Sarah's, Lauren tried to work some more on her newspaper story. But she couldn't keep her mind on it. Her head hurt.

Lauren lay back on her bed. One ear kept listening for the phone to ring. But it didn't. She took off her glasses and closed her eyes. They really burned, like when you get too close to a campfire.

The next thing Lauren knew, her mom was beside her. "Sweetie, do you feel alright?" Her mom touched Lauren's forehead. Her hand felt so nice and cool. "I think you might have some fever."

Lauren did. Almost 102 degrees.

Mom tucked Lauren into bed. And that was where she stayed for the rest of the day. She dozed on and off. Sometimes she'd burrow under her blanket because she was shivering cold. Then she'd throw it off because she was boiling hot.

"Daddy called Dr. Robbins. She says it sounds like flu," Mom told Lauren later. "I think we'll keep you home for a couple of days."

That didn't make Lauren feel any better. Being sick meant being stuck in bed. Bor-ing!

4

The next morning, Lauren woke up expecting to see Mrs. Maguire, who lived down the street. She usually came to baby-sit when Lauren was sick or had a day off from school. But to Lauren's surprise, the first person she saw when she opened her eyes was her mom.

"How come you're home?" Lauren asked, sitting up.

"My partner told me to take the day off," Mom said.

Lauren smiled. Mom's partner was Daddy.

"Besides, the doctor says it's time for me to slow down a little and take it easy."

Lauren sat up in bed and stretched. Her head didn't hurt as much this morning.

"The baby will be here pretty soon," Lauren said, reaching for her glasses. Mom nodded. The date circled on Lauren's wall calendar—"D-Day," it said, for Delivery Day—was only two and a half weeks away.

"Oh, feel," Mom said. She took Lauren's hand and placed it on her tummy.

Right away Lauren felt a thump-thump-thumping inside. It stopped for a moment and then started again. It was like someone knocking at a door.

"Hello in there!" Lauren called to the baby. "I hope you're a girl. But if you're a boy, that's okay. Either way, I can't wait to meet you!"

*　*　*

A little later, Lauren's mom brought a tray and served her breakfast in bed. But Lauren couldn't eat much. Soon her mom took the tray away. When she came back, she had a thick pink book and a shoe box full of pictures.

"I thought it would be fun to look at these," she said. Lauren smiled and reached for her baby book and the box of baby pictures. She slid over in bed to make room for her mom.

"Wow. I can't believe I was ever this little!" Lauren said, as they opened the pink book.

"Lauren—Day 1," it said under a photo of a completely bald baby with a scrunched-up face.

"I look so funny," Lauren said. "Like I smelled something yucky."

There was a lock of hair from Lauren's first haircut—as red then as it was now. And a folded-up piece of paper with a gloppy finger paint design that said, "Lauren's first masterpiece—Age 2." But mostly it was just stuff Mom had written in about her. It was like Lauren's mom thought every move she made was big, exciting, front-page news.

"Lauren smiled her first smile today at three weeks old," it said in Mom's familiar writing.

"Lauren rolled over in her crib!"

"Lauren has started cooing along to the radio."

On and on it went—"Lauren can sit up.... Lauren can crawl.... Lauren can stand...."

"Gee, Mom. You act like no other baby before me ever did any of this stuff."

"That's how it is with a baby. Everything is extra special," Mom explained. "You know, I'm thrilled about this new baby. And I know I'll love it to pieces. But I'll never forget how exciting it was the day you were born. You were a wonderful baby."

After the baby book, Lauren and her mom went through the box of old photos.

"Look at this one!" Mom said, smiling. "It's you and Marsha."

The photo showed Marsha and Lauren together in a sandbox. Lauren seemed to be trying to grab Marsha's shovel. Marsha

looked like she was about to howl in protest.

"You met Marsha before you were even four months old. Marsha was six months old. I remember she seemed so grown-up to me!"

Mom laughed. And Lauren couldn't help giggling, too. Then she looked at the picture again. She hadn't forgotten that Marsha had never called yesterday. But Lauren was sure she would call today after school. They always called each other if one of them was sick. And they always brought over the day's homework assignment with a funny note stuck in it.

But by five o'clock the phone had not rung. Lauren had to find out the day's assignment. But she wasn't going to call Marsha, she decided. After all, she was the one home sick. She'd thought her best friend would at least want to know how she was feeling!

Instead, Lauren called Sarah. The class was learning about synonyms now—words that meant the same thing. Like *small* and *little*. Tonight there was a list of ten words, Sarah told her. And they had to think of a synonym for each one.

Once she had copied down all the words, Lauren asked how Sarah was doing.

"Still sad," Sarah said. "You know, I've decided to write an obituary about Louie for *The Troop Tribune*. But every time I try to write it, it reminds me how much I miss him." Sarah sighed. "Well, bye, Lauren. I've got to do my homework, too. I hope I see you tomorrow in school."

5

But on Tuesday, Lauren's mom kept her home again, even though Lauren felt one hundred percent better. "You know Dr. Robbins's rule—twenty-four hours with no fever."

Actually, it was fun staying home again with Mom. They hardly ever got to spend so much time alone together. "And this may be one of the last times we'll have where it's just the two of us...at least for a while," Mom pointed out as they unpacked a box of Lauren's old baby clothes.

Lauren hadn't really considered that. "The way I figure it," she told her mom, "I've had you and Daddy all to myself for seven and a quarter years! I'm ready to share you guys with somebody else. Really!"

Lauren picked up a tiny pink dress with strawberries all over it. "Oh, this is so cute!" Lauren said. She tried poking her hand through one of the puffed sleeves of the strawberry dress. But it wouldn't fit.

Lauren sat back and held the dress out in front of her. "Mom, do you think friends can outgrow each other?" Maybe, thought Lauren, that was what was happening with Marsha. Maybe Marsha was outgrowing her. Maybe she wanted a friend who was more like a synonym than an antonym.

"Well, people do change," her mom said. "Sometimes they get different interests and go different ways."

Lauren frowned. That wasn't what she wanted to hear.

"But then, look at Jane and me," Mom went on. Jane was her mom's best friend. She had moved to California a long time ago. "Jane's still my best friend, even though we don't get to see each other very often. I love Jane. That hasn't changed. And it never will."

But Lauren was still worried. She knew

her feelings toward her friend hadn't changed. But what about Marsha's?

✳   ✳   ✳

Later that afternoon, the phone rang.

"For you," Mom said, holding out the receiver.

Lauren's face lit up. Marsha! Finally! She grabbed the phone. "Hi!" she said brightly.

"Well, you don't sound one bit sick!"

It was Amy. Not Marsha. A wave of disappointment hit Lauren. But she tried not to let it show in her voice.

"I was sick. But I'm better now. I'll be back in school tomorrow."

"Oh, good! I missed you."

At least somebody had!

"Listen, I'm trying to write my advice column for *The Troop Tribune*," Amy said. "There is only one small problem. Nobody is coming to me with any questions or problems. So I figured I'd better try asking around.... Do you have any problems that 'Dear Amy' can solve?"

Lauren paused for a moment. Amy was smart. Maybe she would have some good advice.

"Well," Lauren said slowly, "I might."

"Oh, great!" Amy said. Then she added quickly, "I didn't mean 'great' that something's bothering you. I meant—"

"Don't worry. I know what you meant," Lauren answered. "Listen, what would you do if you thought a certain friend of yours was mad about something? Only you weren't sure. I mean, maybe that certain friend isn't mad about anything. Maybe she is just getting tired of being your friend. What would you do?"

"Simple. I'd just ask my friend if

anything was bothering her."

"Oh," was all Lauren said.

Of course, what Amy said made sense. But asking stuff like that wasn't easy. Not even with somebody you'd known forever.

"Well...thanks. I guess maybe that's what I'll try to do," Lauren said.

"Great! I'll see you tomorrow." Then Amy giggled. "And thanks. I had no idea giving advice was so easy!"

6

Lauren's dad was late getting her to school the next day. First period had already started. That was when Mrs. Fujikawa let everyone in 2-B do independent activities. They could write in their journals, read a book, and even play board games—as long as they were kind of educational.

When Lauren walked into the classroom, she saw Marsha right away. She and Corrie were playing Battleship.

Marsha looked up for a second. Then she

quickly looked back down at the game.
Lauren felt like going over and shaking her.
She wanted to ask her what had changed
between them. But instead she went over to

her desk. She sat down and took out her
book. And she didn't look up for the rest of
the period.

All morning long, Lauren was sure that
Marsha was ignoring her. And Lauren tried
her best to ignore Marsha right back. But by
lunchtime, she couldn't stand it any longer.

As Lauren came out of the lunch line, she spotted Marsha sitting at a table. She was at the corner where she and Lauren usually sat.

Slowly, Lauren carried her tray over to Marsha.

"Hi," Lauren said. "Okay if I sit here?"

"Okay." Marsha shrugged. She didn't look at Lauren. She just fiddled with the straw of her juice box.

Well, here goes, Lauren thought.

She put her tray down and cleared her throat.

"Marsha, why are you mad at me?" she blurted.

"Who says I'm mad?" Marsha said. She shrugged her shoulders again. But her voice sounded mad. "Of course, it wouldn't have killed you to call me."

"What! Call *you*? *You* should have called *me*!" Lauren's voice was louder than she meant it to be. Kids at other tables were starting to stare at them.

Suddenly Marsha slammed down the lid of her lunchbox. "But I'm the one who's been home sick," she said hotly. "You didn't even call to see how I was!"

Wait a minute! Lauren thought. That was what *she* was supposed to say!

"*You* were sick?" Lauren asked.

"YES, *I* was sick!" Marsha was almost shouting now. "That's why I didn't go to Sarah's house. That's why I haven't been in school for two days. Or didn't you even notice?!"

"How could I?" Lauren shouted back. "*I* was home sick, too!"

Just then, Corrie came by with her tray. "Oops! Guess I'll try another table," she said, and walked away.

For a minute, Lauren and Marsha just looked at each other. Finally, Lauren spoke up. "Listen. I didn't know you were sick," she said.

"Well, same here," said Marsha. "I mean, I didn't know you were sick either." Her voice still didn't sound all that friendly.

Lauren looked down at the slice of pizza on her plate. Marsha stared at her peanut butter sandwich.

They were getting nowhere fast.

Then Lauren thought again about Amy's advice. "Marsha, please," she said. "Won't you tell me what you're really mad about? I know something's bothering you."

Marsha finally looked Lauren in the eyes.

"Well...I'm not mad exactly," Marsha said slowly. She heaved a sigh.

Lauren waited for her to continue. She was trying her hardest to be patient and not hurry her.

"Okay. I know this will sound silly," Marsha went on. "But all you talk about is the baby. The baby this. And the baby that. How you can't wait to read to the baby. And how much fun it'll be to give the baby a bottle and push the baby in the stroller." Marsha sighed again. "Maybe my mom is right. She says I'm jealous. And maybe I am."

"Jealous?"

Marsha bit her lip. "The baby isn't even born yet and already we don't spend as much time together. I'm worried that when the baby comes, you really won't have time for me." Marsha turned her face away. "You've never had a brother or sister. And I know you're excited about it. But I always felt kind of like *I* was the closest thing you had to a sister. Now that's going to change."

"Oh, Marsha! And I was scared that you didn't want to be best friends anymore." Lauren stood up, reached across the table, and flung her arms around Marsha. "I was jealous, too. I saw you playing in the tree house with Jo Ann. And that made me feel bad."

Lauren released Marsha from her hug. Some pizza cheese had gotten on her shirt. But who cared? "Listen, Marsh. The baby

will be my sister or brother—and I hope it's
my sister," Lauren added for good luck.
"But you are my best, best friend. And
that's the way I want it to be forever and
ever and ever and ever and—"

"Okay, okay! I get the point," Marsha
said fondly.

"Hey, you guys. Is it safe to sit here
now?" Amy walked up to them with her
lunch tray. "Anything I can help you with?"

Lauren laughed and pulled out a chair for
Amy. "No, 'Dear Amy.' Everything's just
fine now! Just great!"

7

On Thursday, when Lauren got home from school, both her mother and father were waiting for her in the living room.

"How come you're home so early, Dad?" Lauren asked. Then Lauren noticed a suitcase next to her mother's chair.

Mom smiled a funny smile.

Lauren's mouth fell open. "The baby's going to be born, isn't it?"

Mom nodded.

"But it's two weeks early!" Lauren said, worried.

"Babies have a way of coming when they want to. You were an early arrival, too—always in a hurry," Dad said with a smile.

Lauren wrapped herself around her mother's neck. Her heart was pounding. "Mom, I'm nervous!"

"That makes two of us." Mom hugged Lauren hard. "But everything will be fine. We're just having a little trouble finding a baby-sitter to come stay with you."

They had planned for Mrs. Maguire to

53

come. But she was visiting her grandchildren this week.

"Hey! I know where I can stay," Lauren said.

All it took was a phone call.

* * *

Lauren's parents dropped her off at Marsha's house on the way to the hospital.

"We'll call as soon as we have news!" Lauren's dad promised.

Lauren reached over and patted her mom's tummy one last time. "See you soon!" she told the baby.

And as Lauren climbed out of the car, it hit her. The next time she saw her parents, there was going to be a brand-new person in this world. And she was going to be that brand-new person's big sister.

Waiting for anything was never easy for Lauren. But this was torture. She couldn't keep her mind on anything—not TV, not Monopoly.

It was Marsha's idea to set up an obstacle course in the big backyard. "We have got to take your mind off this," she said.

"Yes!" Lauren agreed. A big project was just what she needed.

The obstacle course was fun. And best of all, tiring. By the third time through, Lauren was totally pooped. But it felt good. She couldn't think or worry while she was wriggling through Marsha's tire swing or racing across the monkey bars.

It was such a warm night that Marsha's mother let the girls sleep in the tree house. They took sleeping bags and pillows and two flashlights and stretched out on the carpeted floor.

"I bet I won't sleep a wink," Lauren whispered. Through the tree branches she could see the stars winking at her. And the lights on inside Marsha's house gave her a safe, cozy feeling.

"I'll stay up, too, if you can't sleep. I promise," Marsha said. Then she let out a yawn. "Oops! Pretend I didn't do that!"

"I am really glad I'm here with you and not at home with Mrs. Maguire," Lauren told her.

"Gosh, the baby will *really* be here soon—I can't believe it. I sure hope it's a girl," she went on, "but—"

"'If it's a boy, I'll still be happy.'" Marsha finished the sentence for Lauren.

Lauren giggled. "Sorry. We can talk about something else."

"No. It's okay. I hope it's a little girl, too. With red hair just like you." Marsha leaned over and squeezed Lauren's hand. "I'm excited, too."

Lauren squeezed back. "Thanks." Marsha really was the best friend ever!

✻ ✻ ✻

"Lauren! Lauren! Your father's on the phone!" Marsha's father called up from the base of the tree.

By some miracle Lauren had fallen asleep. But now she bolted upright in her sleeping bag.

"I'm coming," Lauren croaked.

Lauren crawled over Marsha who was dead asleep. Then she scrambled down the tree and flew toward the house.

At last, she'd find out. Did she have a little brother? Or—Lauren crossed her fingers—a little sister? She took the phone from Marsha's mother's hand.

"Daddy! How's Mommy and the baby?" she cried. "Is it a boy or a girl?"

* * *

"My lips are sealed," Marsha said the next day at the Friday after-school Brownie meeting. "Lauren wants to tell everybody herself." If Marsha had said this once, she must have said it one hundred times today.

"Oh, come on, Marsha!" several Brownies complained.

"Now girls, give Marsha a break!" Mrs.

Q. said. "Lauren should be here soon." She clapped her hands as if that put an end to the discussion. "Now let's get down to business. Who remembered to bring in an article for *The Troop Tribune?*"

Nearly all the Brownie Girl Scouts raised their hands.

"Very good! Does anyone want to share what they've written with us?" Mrs. Q. looked around the room. "How about you, Marsha?"

Marsha read her story. It was about meeting Violetta Jamison, the world-famous ballerina. "It never would have happened if

it weren't for Lauren and the rest of my Brownie friends. The end," Marsha said.

Next Krissy A. showed everybody a crossword puzzle that she had made. All the clues were about Girl Scouting.

Corrie showed them the comic strip she had drawn about a girl named "Ima Brownie."

Then Sarah read her obituary for Louie. "Amy's dad helped me with the kind of stuff I needed to put in." Sarah cleared her throat and began to read. "Louie, a hamster aged nine months, died last Sunday. He lived at 32 Shady Acres. Louie was a loving pet. He liked eating Cheerios, running on his wheel, and being petted. He leaves behind two hamsters, Huey and Dewey, a puppy named Muffin, a cat named Norma, seven tropical fish, and his owner, Sarah—"

Sarah's words were cut off as Lauren

burst through the swinging doors of the
lunchroom.

"I'm a sister!" she exclaimed.

Everyone swarmed around her.

"We know! We know!" they shouted.
"So tell us! Is it a girl or a boy?"

Lauren cleared her throat and grinned.
"It's . . . a girl!"

A cheer rang through the lunchroom.

Then Lauren reported as best she could. She had gotten only a short peek at the baby. It was through the glass window of the hospital nursery. "To tell the truth, a lot of the babies all looked alike to me. The only way I knew it was my sister—" Lauren paused. It felt so great saying the word sister! "—was from the little sign on the bassinet."

"This is wonderful news!" Mrs. Q. said. She came up and hugged Lauren. "Perfect for *The Troop Tribune*."

News! Lauren looked at all the stories spread out on the lunch table.

"Oops! I forgot to bring my story in," she said. "But I think I know just what to say."

Lauren sat down and quickly wrote out her story. When she was done, she shared it with the troop—who all agreed it would go on page one.

Future Brownie Girl Scout Is Born

My mother had a baby girl last night at 11:22 exactly. She weighs almost nine pounds. That is very big for a baby. She does not have a first name yet. She does not have any hair yet.

Yesterday there were only three people in my family. Today there are four! And I am a sister!

What will it be like?
I don't know.
But I am very excited!

Girl Scout Ways

Looking over her baby book and old baby pictures with her mom made Lauren's sick day lots more fun. You can have fun, too, looking at old photos with your family and friends. Or you can use them to make a special book all about YOU!

- To make your own book, you will need: 8½ x 11 construction paper, 5½ x 8½ writing paper, a stapler, markers or crayons, tape, glue or glue stick, photos of you, your family, and friends. (Make sure it's okay for you to use them in your book before you start.)

- Fold construction paper in half. This will be your cover.

- Staple writing paper to inside of cover. These will be your inside pages.

- Decorate the cover with a photo or drawing of you.

- Fill each inside page with information about you. Here are some ideas:

  Include photos of you at different ages and in different places. Write in funny captions.

  Make a time line. Write in important events in your life—like your first day of school or the first time you lost a tooth.

- Share your special book with old friends and new, and keep adding to it as you get older.